Max Goes to the Barber

by Adria F. Klein
illustrated by Mernie Gallagher-Cole

Special thanks to our advisers for their expertise:

Adria F. Klein, Ph.D.
Professor Emeritus, California State University
San Bernardino, California

Susan Kesselring, M.A., Literacy Educator
Rosemount–Apple Valley–Eagan (Minnesota) School District

Max likes to go to the barber shop.

A Note to Parents and Caregivers:

Read-it! Readers are for children who are just starting on the amazing road to reading. These beautiful books support both the acquisition of reading skills and the love of books.

The PURPLE LEVEL presents basic topics and objects using high frequency words and simple language patterns.

The RED LEVEL presents familiar topics using common words and repeating sentence patterns.

The BLUE LEVEL presents new ideas using a larger vocabulary and varied sentence structure.

The YELLOW LEVEL presents more challenging ideas, a broad vocabulary, and wide variety in sentence structure.

The GREEN LEVEL presents more complex ideas, an extended vocabulary range, and expanded language structures.

The ORANGE LEVEL presents a wide range of ideas and concepts using challenging vocabulary and complex language structures.

When sharing a book with your child, read in short stretches, pausing often to talk about the pictures. Have your child turn the pages and point to the pictures and familiar words. And be sure to reread favorite stories or parts of stories.

There is no right or wrong way to share books with children. Find time to read with your child, and pass on the legacy of literacy.

Adria F. Klein, Ph.D.
Professor Emeritus
California State University
San Bernardino, California

Editor: Jacqueline A. Wolfe
Page Production: Amy Bailey Muehlenhardt
Creative Director: Keith Griffin
Editorial Director: Carol Jones
Managing Editor: Catherine Neitge
The illustrations in this book were created with watercolor and colored pencil.

Picture Window Books
A Capstone Imprint
1710 Roe Crest Drive
North Mankato, MN 56003
www.capstonepub.com

Library of Congress Cataloging-in-Publication Data
Klein, Adria F.
Max goes to the barber / by Adria F. Klein; illustrated by
Mernie Gallagher-Cole.
p. cm. — (Read-it! readers)
Summary: During a visit to the barber, Max gets his hair cut and combed.
ISBN 13: 978-1-4048-1180-5 (library binding)
ISBN 13: 978-1-4048-3060-8 (paperback)
[1. Haircutting—Fiction. 2. Hispanic Americans—Fiction.] I. Gallagher-Cole,
Mernie, ill. II. Title. III. Series.

PZ7.K678324Mam 2005 2005003851
[E]—dc22

Printed and bound in the United States of America.
031519 001762

Shop
217
218
Barbe

Max goes to the barber shop when he needs a haircut.

He meets the barber.

He sits in the chair. The barber puts a cape on Max.

HAIR
Shampoo
with
Aloe

The barber combs Max's hair.

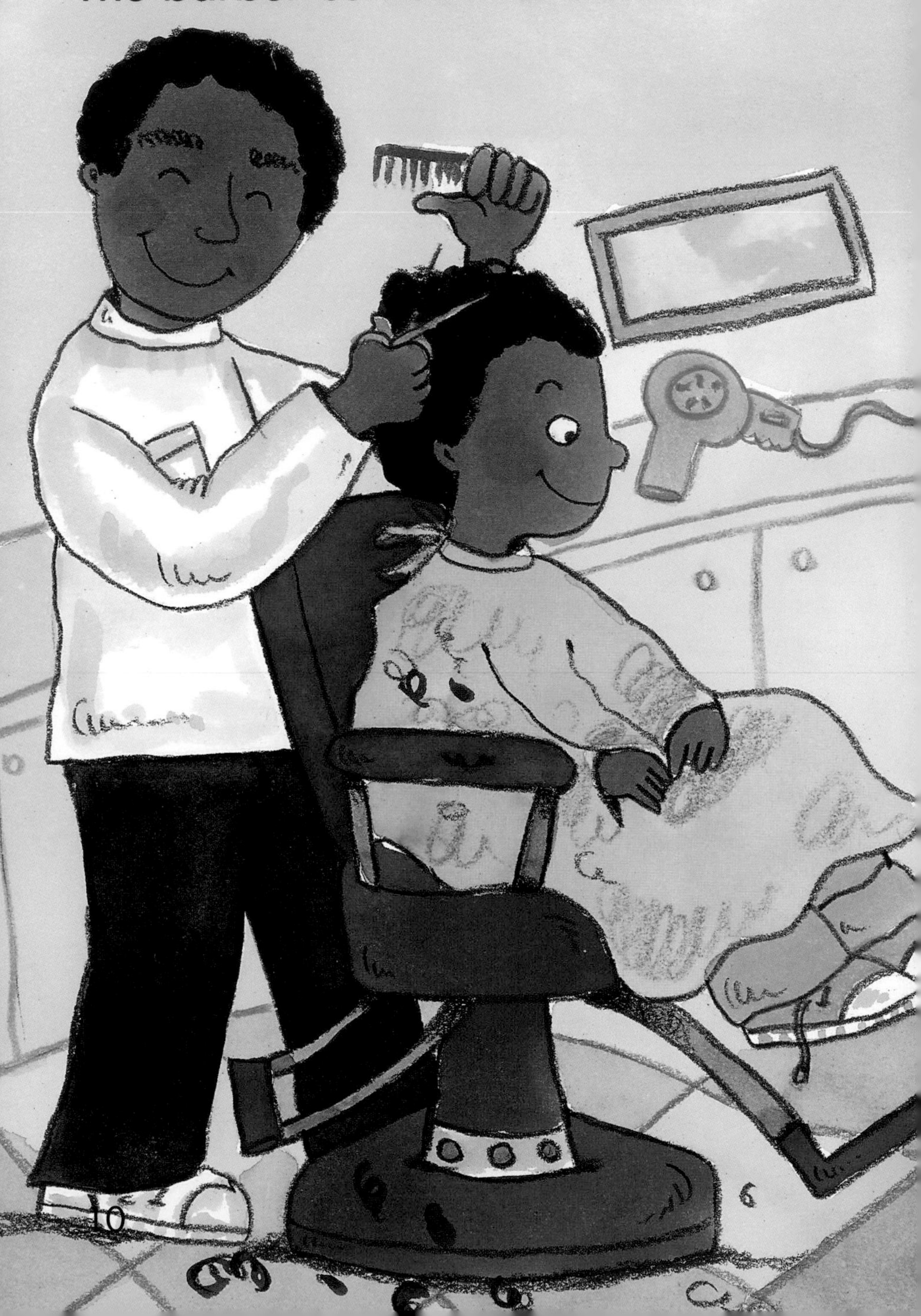

The barber cuts the hair on the top of Max's head.

The barber cuts the hair on the side of Max's head.

The barber cuts the hair on the back of Max's head.

The barber brushes the cut hair off of Max.

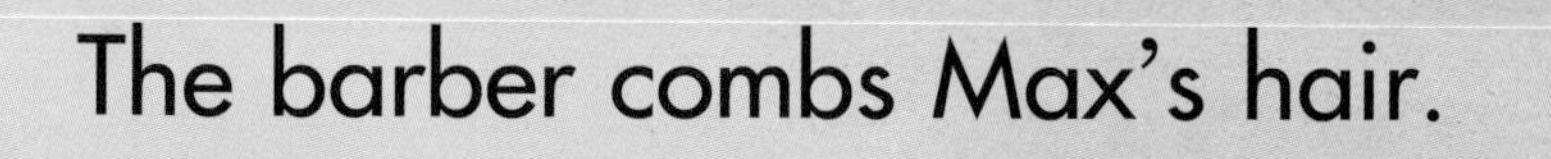
The barber combs Max's hair.

Max looks in the mirror.

The barber gives Max a comb.

Max wants to come back to the barber shop very soon.

Barber
HOURS

Max likes his new haircut.

Max likes to go to the barber shop.

WAIT!
DON'T CLOSE THE BOOK!
capstone kids .com
THERE'S MORE!

FIND MORE:

Games & Puzzles
Heroes & Villains
Authors & Illustrators
AT...